D0568105

DRAT THAT FAT CAT!

By **Pat Thomson**

Illustrated by **Ailie Busby**

Arthur A. Levine Books

AN IMPRINT OF SCHOLASTIC PRESS

For Rosalind and Alexandra, and Grandma too.
—P.T.

With very special thanks to Ness.
—A.B.

Text copyright © 2003 by Pat Thomson • Illustrations copyright © 2003 by Ailie Busby • All rights reserved. Published by Scholastic Press, a division of Scholastic Inc., *Publishers since 1920*, by arrangement with Scholastic Children's Books, a division of Scholastic Ltd (UK). SCHOLASTIC, SCHOLASTIC PRESS and the LANTERN LOGO are trademarks and/or registered trademarks of Scholastic Inc.

No part of this publication may be reproduced, or stored in a retrieval system, or transmitted in any form or by any means, electronic, mechanical, photocopying, recording, or otherwise, without written permission of the publisher. For information regarding permission, write to Scholastic Ltd., Attention: Permissions Department,Commonwealth House, 1-19 New Oxford Street, London WCIA INU

Library of Congress Cataloging-in-Publication Data

Thomson, Pat.
Drat that fat cat! / by Pat Thomson ; illustrated by Ailie Busby.—1st ed. p. cm.
Summary: A fat cat in search of food eats up everything he meets until he swallows a bee.

ISBN 0-439-47195-8

[1. Cats—Fiction. 2. Animals—Fiction.] I. Busby, Ailie, ill. II. Title.
PZ7.T3765 Dr 2003 [E]—dc21 2002008888

1 3 5 7 9 10 8 6 4 2   03 04 05 06 07

Printed in Dubai, UAE
First American edition, November 2003

The display type was set in MotterCorpus.
The text type was set in Leawood Book 20-point.
Book design by Yvette Awad

Once there was a cat, a fat, fat cat. But was that cat fat enough?

No,
he was
not!

So he padded along
the path in search of food.

The fat cat met a rat.

"Have you any food, rat, deep in your hole?"

"No, I have not," said the rat.

"Too bad, then. I must eat *you* up."

"Eat *me* up? You are fat
enough already!"

But was that cat fat enough?

No,
he was
not!

So he gobbled up the rat and padded along
the path in search of food, with the rat
squeak, squeak, squeaking inside him.

The fat cat met a duck.
"Have you any food, duck,
to nibble in your nest?"
"No, I have not," said the duck.
"Too bad, then. I must eat *you* up."
"Eat *me* up? You are fat enough already!"

But was that cat fat enough?

No, he was not!

So he gobbled up the duck and padded along the path in search of food, with the duck **quack**, **quack**, **quacking** and the rat squeak, squeak, squeaking inside him.

The fat cat met a dog.
"Have you any food, dog,
hidden in your house?"
"No, I have not," said the dog.
"Too bad, then. I must eat *you* up."
"Eat *me* up? You are fat enough already!"

But was that cat fat enough?

No,
he was
not!

So he gobbled up the dog and padded along the path in search of food, with the dog **woof, woof, woofing,** the duck **quack, quack, quacking,** and the rat squeak, squeak, squeaking inside him.

The fat cat met an old lady.
"Have you any food, old lady,
at the bottom of your basket?"
"No, I have not," said the old lady.
"Too bad, then. I must eat *you* up."
"Eat *me* up? You are fat enough already!"

But was that cat fat enough?

No, he was not!

So he gobbled up the old lady and padded along the path in search of food, with the old lady saying **"Drat that fat cat!"**, the dog **woof, woof, woofing**, the duck **quack, quack, quacking**, and the rat **squeak, squeak, squeaking** inside him.

A bee buzzed around the fat cat's head and,
without a thought,
he swallowed it. . . .

Whole!

The bee buzzed around inside the fat cat,
where he found a rat squeak, squeak, squeaking,
a duck **quack, quack, quacking**,
a dog **woof, woof, woofing**,
and an old lady saying

"**Drat that fat cat!**"

Squeak!

"This is an outrage!" buzzed the bee.
"There isn't room to swing a *cat* in here."

The fat cat had forgotten that bees sting.
"Ow!" cried the fat cat.

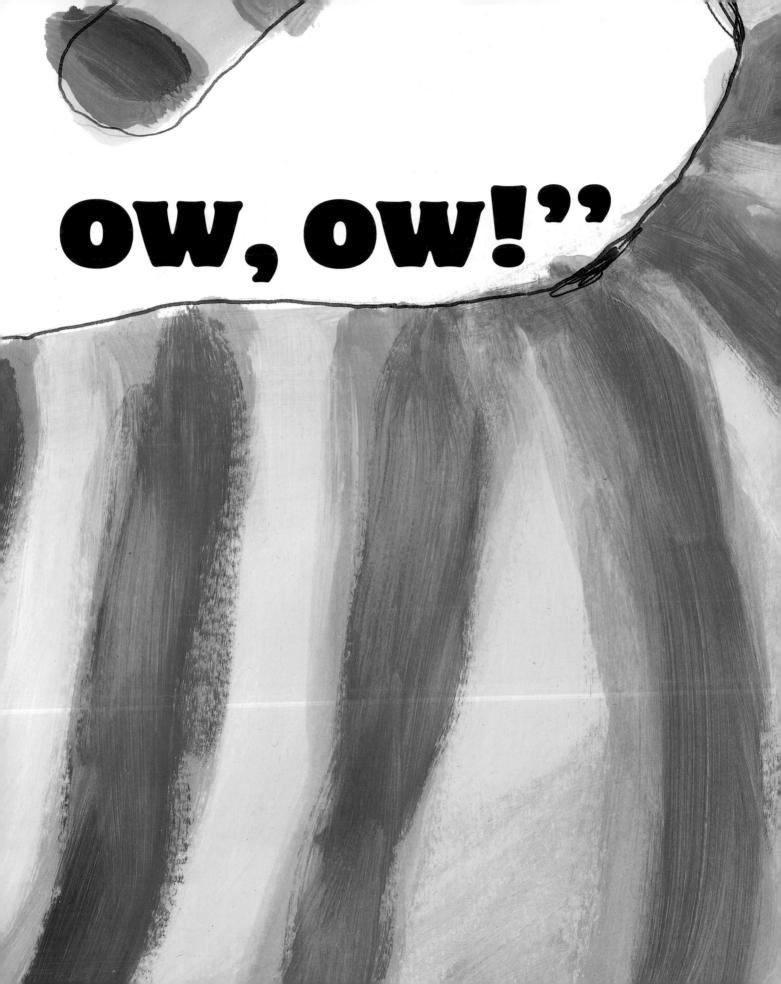

Hic! went the cat and
out popped the bee.

Hic! went the
cat and out
popped
the rat.

Hic! went
the cat and
out popped
the duck.

Hic! went the cat and out popped the dog.

Hic! went the cat and out popped the old lady.

"Dear me," said the old lady,
"you must be very hungry.
Come home with me and
I'll fatten you up."

The cat padded along
the path behind her,
in search of food,
hic, hic, hiccing
all the way home.

So was that cat now fat enough?

lo, he

vas not!

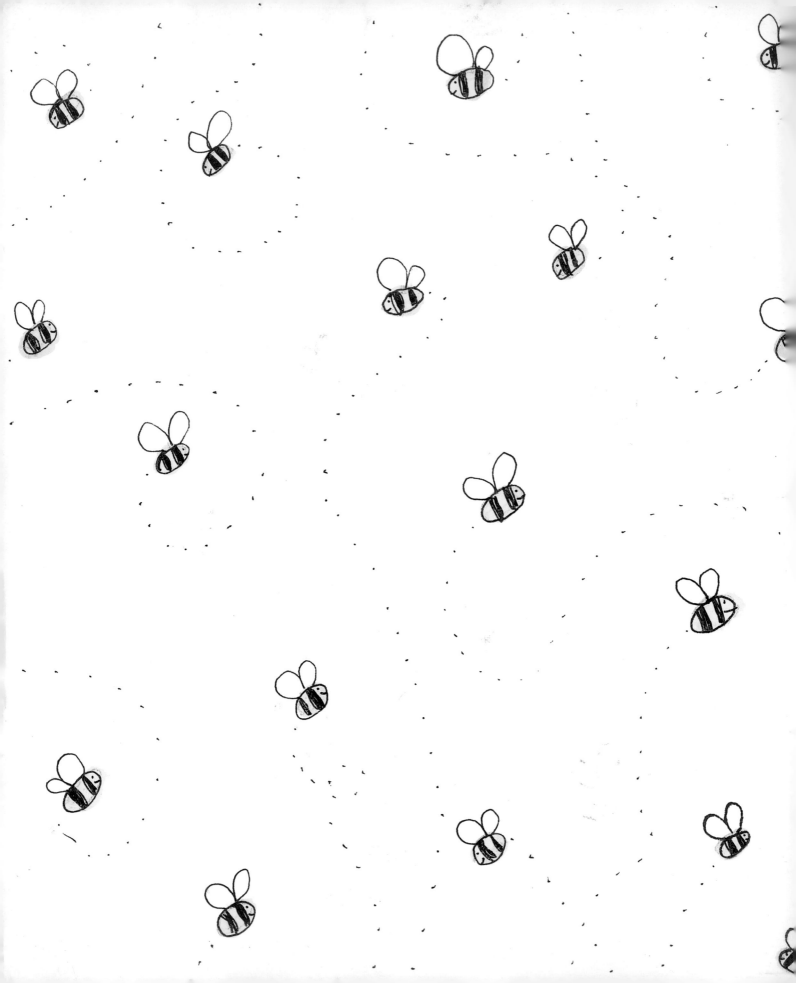